Dear Parents and Educators,

Welcome to Penguin Young Readers! As parents and educators, you know that each child develops at his or her own pace—in terms of speech, critical thinking, and, of course, reading. Penguin Young Readers recognizes this fact. As a result, each Penguin Young Readers book is assigned a traditional easy-to-read level (1–4) as well as a Guided Reading Level (A–P). Both of these systems will help you choose the right book for your child. Please refer to the back of each book for specific leveling information. Penguin Young Readers features esteemed authors and illustrators, stories about favorite characters, fascinating nonfiction, and more!

| Kit and Kat | LEVEL **2** GUIDED READING LEVEL **E** |

This book is perfect for a **Progressing Reader** who:
• can figure out unknown words by using picture and context clues;
• can recognize beginning, middle, and ending sounds;
• can make and confirm predictions about what will happen in the text; and
• can distinguish between fiction and nonfiction.

Here are some **activities** you can do during and after reading this book:
• Make Predictions: What do you think will happen if Tom acts like a bully again? What will Kit and Kat do? Act out a scene to demonstrate this.
• Sight Words: Sight words are frequently used words that readers must know just by looking at them. These words are not "sounded out" or "decoded"; rather they are known instantly, on sight. Knowing these words helps children develop into efficient readers. Reread the story and have the child point out the sight words listed below.

could	got	now	soon	was
find	had	off	their	went
game	her	out	they	were
going	his	over	two	your

Remember, sharing the love of reading with a child is the best gift you can give!

—Bonnie Bader, EdM, and Katie Carella, EdM
    Penguin Young Readers program

*Penguin Young Readers are leveled by independent reviewers applying the standards developed by Irene Fountas and Gay Su Pinnell in *Matching Books to Readers: Using Leveled Books in Guided Reading*, Heinemann, 1999.

Developed by The Philip Lief Group, Inc.

Penguin Young Readers
Published by the Penguin Group
Penguin Group (USA) Inc., 375 Hudson Street, New York, New York 10014, USA
Penguin Group (Canada), 90 Eglinton Avenue East, Suite 700, Toronto, Ontario M4P 2Y3, Canada
(a division of Pearson Penguin Canada Inc.)
Penguin Books Ltd., 80 Strand, London WC2R 0RL, England
Penguin Group Ireland, 25 St. Stephen's Green, Dublin 2, Ireland (a division of Penguin Books Ltd.)
Penguin Group (Australia), 250 Camberwell Road, Camberwell, Victoria 3124, Australia
(a division of Pearson Australia Group Pty. Ltd.)
Penguin Books India Pvt. Ltd., 11 Community Centre, Panchsheel Park, New Delhi—110 017, India
Penguin Group (NZ), 67 Apollo Drive, Rosedale, Auckland 0632, New Zealand
(a division of Pearson New Zealand Ltd.)
Penguin Books (South Africa) (Pty.) Ltd., 24 Sturdee Avenue,
Rosebank, Johannesburg 2196, South Africa

Penguin Books Ltd., Registered Offices: 80 Strand, London WC2R 0RL, England

Library of Congress Control Number: 94015070

ISBN 978-0-448-40748-7   10 9 8 7 6 5 4 3 2 1

Kit and Kat

by Tomie dePaola

Penguin Young Readers
An Imprint of Penguin Group (USA) Inc.

Kit's Pajamas

Today was a big day

for Kit and Kat.

They were going to sleep at

Grandma and Grandpa's house.

Kit and Kat got out their stuff.

Soon they were ready.

"Do you have everything?"

asked Grandma.

"Yes," said Kit.

"Yes," said Kat.

So off they went.

Kit and Kat had fun.

Grandpa gave the best rides.

Grandma read the best stories.

Soon it was time for bed.

Kat put on her pajamas.

But Kit could not find his.

"I left them at home!"

said Kit.

And he began to cry.

"Don't cry," said Grandpa.

"Look!"

"Oh, Grandpa," said Kit.

"Your pajama top!"

"You look like

a little Grandpa,"

said Kat.

Then they both went to sleep.

Kat's Good Idea

One day, Kit and Kat

got a big surprise

from Mom and Dad.

Two bikes!

Kat got a red bike.

Kit got a blue bike.

"Let's race!" said Kat.

She got on the red bike.

Off she went.

"I WIN!" said Kat.

Kit got on the blue bike.

But he did not move.

"I am too little," he said.

"My feet do not reach

the pedals."

Kat had an idea.

She got two blocks.

Kat put the blocks

on the pedals.

"Your feet will reach now,"

said Kat.

Then Kit got on his bike.

His feet **did** reach!

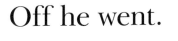

Off he went.

"I WIN!" said Kit

to Kat.

Kit, Kat, and the Bully

Kit and Kat were having fun.

They were playing with blocks.

Then Tom came over.

Tom was no fun.

What did Tom do?

He kicked the blocks.

"Blocks are for babies,"

said Tom.

Then Tom said,

"Let's go on the seesaw.

The seesaw is fun."

But the seesaw

was no fun—

not with Tom.

"Now I want to ride
in your car," said Tom.
"But you are too big,"
said Kat.
"No, I'm not!"
said Tom.

Tom got in.

He **was** too big.

He got stuck.

"Help!" cried Tom.

"Help! Help!"

"Say the magic word," said Kat.

"Please," said Tom.

But that was not enough.

"Pretty please," said Tom.

But that was not enough.

"Pretty please with sugar
on top," said Tom.

That was enough.

Kit and Kat pulled Tom
out of the car.

And Tom did not

act like a bully—

for the rest of that day!